GEORGESS McHARGUE
Funny Bananas
THE MYSTERY IN THE MUSEUM

Illustrated by Heidi Palmer

Holt, Rinehart and Winston
New York   Chicago   San Francisco

78-30

Library of Congress Cataloging in Publication Data

McHargue, Georgess.
    Funny bananas; the mystery in the museum.

    SUMMARY: Ben's efforts to apprehend the vandal plaguing
the natural history museum are complicated by a "witch" and a
strange animal who seem to be haunting the museum.
    [1. Mystery and detective stories. 2. Museums—Fiction] I. Pal-
mer, Heidi, illus. II. Title.
PZ7.M183Fu   [Fic]   74-17259
ISBN 0-03-013761-6

● ●

For Kelly and Traci
with love from the W.S.

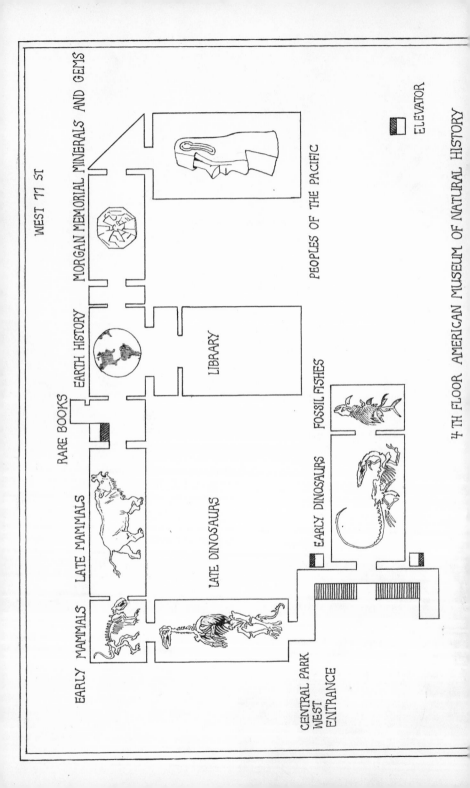

1

"Hey, Ben, watch out for the charging elephants!"

"It's all right. I'm in a Land-Rover." Ben answered without turning around. He was intent on the herd of African elephants that was thundering down on him from only twenty feet away, trunks raised and tusks waving. As usual, he wished they were real instead of mounted specimens in a museum hall. Not that the museum wasn't great. He turned and grinned up at his friend Al, the museum guard. "I was filming them, till the dust got too thick," he explained. "What are you doing down here instead of in Fishes?"

Al was a tall, stretched-looking man in his late sixties who looked like a retired sailor but had actually spent his younger years running a pizza parlor in Coney Island.

"Never was closer to a fish than a large pizza with anchovies," he used to say; "not till the day I went broke and the museum took me on and started me out in Marine Fishes. That was the old hall, of course."

Now Al looked out at the slowly circling crowd in the hall of African Mammals and shrugged his pointed shoulders. "Aw, I probably shouldn't tell you this," he said, "but they had a little trouble down here around noon. Sent me down to substitute. Seems one of the other guards, a new guy, might have had a drop too much to drink. Seeing things, you know what I mean?"

Ben nodded, but he really wasn't interested. Even he, who liked to think he knew more about the museum than anybody, didn't know all the dozens of guards there. Often, new guards didn't stay long enough for him to get to know them, so he just visited his special friends, like Al, or Charley in Late Dinosaurs.

The museum was Ben Pollock's playground, and had been for as long as he could remember. Both his parents worked in the scientific part of the museum, and as his mother sometimes said, "We just let the museum be our baby-sitter." That was fine with Ben. Most kids aren't so lucky as to have Great Blue Whales, brontosauruses, and ancient Aztecs for baby-sitters. Ben picked up his notebook and went off to finish the drawing of a horse skeleton he was making for science class.

Two evenings later, Ben's father looked up from his newspaper and asked, "What's this in the *Times* about vandalism in the museum? In one of the bird halls, it says. Did you hear anything about it, Charlotte?"

Ben's mother lowered her book and said, "Not a thing.

It can't have been very serious or the whole place would have been buzzing."

Ben stopped reviewing the Six Causes of the Civil War. Anything about the museum was his business too. "I was up on Four today," he said, "but Charley didn't say anything about that. What's vandalism anyhow?"

"It's damaging and breaking things for no reason, Ben," explained his mother. "It's like writing on walls or smashing windshields. Go on, dear, what else does it say?"

"Not much. It's only a very small item. It just says some damage was done and police are investigating. Part of one of the exhibits was broken into, I gather, but nothing was taken. Ross will be upset, and the President too. If it can happen once, it can happen again."

Ben went straight to the museum after school, not even stopping at home for his usual pocketful of fig newtons. He found the site of the vandalism in the hall called Birds of the World, on the second floor. Big wooden screens had been moved into place around one of the cases, but that didn't stop Ben. He walked purposefully around to a drab-looking door near the entrance of the hall, opened it, and followed a dim corridor that ran behind the big, lighted cases showing exotic birds in their native habitat. The back of one of the cases was open and two men were standing beside it. "Hi," said Ben cheerfully, and before they could tell him that visitors were not allowed in this area he added, "I'm Ben Pollock and Dr. Ross said I could come and look. I spend a lot of time around here. Do you think you could tell me what happened?"

The young curator sighed and shook his head. The other man looked at Ben over the top of his glasses and asked, "Say, aren't you Dr. Pollock's kid? I've seen you around in the labs over there, I think."

Ben was edging between the two men, trying to get a good view of the damaged exhibit. "That's right," he said, grinning. "That is, it's half right."

"Huh? Wait a minute. How can you be half somebody's son?"

"Oh, It's not half of me, it's two of them."

Now both men were looking at him as if he had turned green and sprouted feathers. Ben was enjoying himself. "You see," he explained, "my *mother's* Dr. *Charlotte* Pollock. She does things with hoofed mammals. And my *dad* is Dr. *Marcus* Pollock. He's a visiting researcher in geology. So one Dr. Pollock is only half right. *I'm* going to be a wildlife photographer, so I sort of take an interest in everything. Like this, for instance. Do you know who did it yet?"

"Good lord," chuckled the curator. "The poor kid's got museumitis from both sides of the family. All right, Ben. I'm Dr. Di Novo and this is Mr. Jackson. Come and see what we've got. Only I warn you, it isn't much."

Indeed, when Ben looked inside the case, he could hardly tell at first what was wrong. The display showed several different kinds of jungle fowl and small birds of southern Asia. Every detail of the mounted birds and their forest home was copied with the greatest care from real life, Ben knew. Not a leaf or flower, feather or branch was wrong for the place, the season, and the time of day shown on the painted backdrop. Only, in one corner, one of the branches of a large bush had been broken off, a heavy rock had been turned over, and the dead leaves and little plants of the forest floor had been scraped up or trampled.

"Now look at this," commanded Mr. Jackson. "That was a very nice *Gallus gallus*—the wild red jungle fowl." He showed Ben a small table in the corridor. On it was a pile of coppery feathers that had once been a beautifully mounted bird resembling a wild rooster. Now the tail was badly draggled, one wing had been torn off, and most of the feathers were gone from one side of the neck.

"My gosh," said Ben, "what a mean thing to do. That old bird wasn't hurting anything."

"No," agreed Mr. Jackson, "and I'm afraid it's ruined, too. Major feathers broken. Of course, it's not what you'd call a *very rare* bird, but we don't happen to have another one on hand at the moment and I don't know where we can get one, unless from another museum. Even if we repair the plants and the scenery, it leaves a big hole in the display without it."

"What I don't get is how they got in here," said Ben. "I mean, they must have come in through this corridor and then opened the back of the case. But most people don't even know this is here. Except us museum people, of course. Besides, it's locked except when somebody's in here. And how could they have done it at all, with everybody looking in through the glass?"

Mr. Jackson was packing the damaged bird into a cardboard box. "Oh, they didn't do it in the daytime. We know that, at least. The custodian came in on his regular check after closing and everything was fine. He's sure of that. But there's something else—something they didn't report in the papers. I guess it seemed too pointless. The same night this happened, somebody went to the big information desk in the main hall and just tore it apart.

10

Pamphlets and leaflets and maps of the museum scattered all over. Everything all mixed up, but nothing taken. Even the wastebasket was dumped out. Now you just explain that. And say, would you mind putting your finger on the string?"

"But that's crazy!" Ben exclaimed, obediently holding the string. "I mean, it's really weird. Why would anybody do that? It's dumb. When do you think the police will catch them?" he added hopefully.

Dr. Di Novo finished closing the back of the case. "Honestly, Ben," he said, "I doubt that they will. You see, they're pretty busy in a city like New York. And really, no important damage was done. It just means some work for Arthur and me, and of course the volunteers who work at the information desk. Nobody was hurt and nothing was stolen, so although the police will keep an eye on the place for a while, they probably think they have more important things to do than track down a bird vandal."

More important? Ben was insulted. "Huh," he said resentfully. "That's all *they* know. If they won't find out who did it, *I will*."

"Terrific," commented Mr. Jackson over his shoulder. "You do that, Ben, and I wish you all kinds of luck. Let me know when you find him, and I'll even punch the guy in the nose for you. He's sure given us a lot of trouble. The thing that really bothers me, though, is that if it could happen once, it can happen again. Are you ready, Doctor? We've still got that report to write."

With a "See you around, Ben," the two men headed down the corridor toward the museum offices in another wing of the building.

That same evening, it did happen again. That was what the Pollock family learned when the telephone rang just as Ben was leaving for school the next morning. "*Well*," said Ben's mother, hanging up the phone, "this time they've stolen something. Or should I say kidnapped?"

"Kidnapped!" demanded Ben and his father in the same breath, and Ben added, "Oh, Mom, *tell me fast* or I'll miss the bus."

"Ben, don't get all excited. I was kidding, really. Susan Markin called to say she went in early and found a terrible mess in the offices of the insect department. Things pushed off desks, and so on. It wasn't till she went in to telephone the security man that she noticed Ruthie was gone."

"Ruthie?" said Ben's father incredulously. "You don't mean Carson's pet spider?"

"Yes, I do. The tarantula. The wire was off the cage and it was empty. Susan says she hopes whoever took it took it far away. She'd rather go for a swim with a tiger shark, even if Carson does say tarantulas make charming pets. That's all I know, Ben-boy, so run along. If you don't have hockey practice today, come up to my workroom after school and I'll tell you what else develops."

2

Ben *did* have field hockey practice that afternoon, and it didn't go any better than the rest of the day had gone. He'd messed up a set of prints in the darkroom, been late for math, and forgotten to return three library books. Now this.

"Pollock!" yelled Mr. Freeman, the coach, "what do you think this is, a nature walk? You could have taken that ball away from Willis six times at least."

Even his best friend Gene looked at him sadly and asked, "What's the matter with you, old buddy? All day you've been acting like you've got rocks in your head."

"Not rocks," muttered Ben, "spiders. Also jungle fowl, and vandals."

Luckily, the next day was Saturday. Ben was at the

museum entrance even before the building opened at ten o'clock. Of course, he could have gotten in earlier by going around through the office and administrative wing, which is not open to the public. On this day, however, Ben was not interested in the exhibits. He was interested in the visitors.

It was like any other Saturday at the museum—people, people, and more people. Through the two big entrances on Central Park West and Seventy-seventh Street came babies, bankers, and Boy Scouts, professors, policemen, and poets, students and steelworkers, tourists and taxicab drivers, lovers and little old ladies. Some stayed ten minutes and some stayed all day. Some knew exactly what they wanted to see and some wandered aimlessly. They ate in the cafeteria, bought things in the museum shop, watched films, heard lectures, and mostly just looked. As the day went on, children got lost, jackets got left behind, feet got tired. The guards were asked thousands of questions and were able to answer an amazing number of them. Through all this wandered Ben Pollock.

He began by looking suspiciously at every single person, but that was obviously an impossible way to do things. What does a museum vandal look like, anyway? After only a little while, Ben found that even pregnant women in blue coats, four-year-olds in overalls, and elderly people in wheelchairs looked as if they were up to no good.

Ben was getting nowhere. Discouraged, he went down to the cafeteria for a tuna fish sandwich. He had been hoping to have a chat with his friend Mrs. Tito, who worked there. However, it seemed to be her day off. He went gloomily back upstairs, hoping to cheer himself up by looking at the Asiatic mammals. He was especially fond of the Siberian tiger.

Of course, there were many other things Ben could have done with his Saturday. He could have gone home and telephoned Gene or one of his other pals. He could have taken his treasured camera and gone looking for good people-pictures in the park. He could have worked on his wildlife stamp collection, or gone with his mother, who had been called out to the Bronx Zoo to look at a rare Chinese deer, or even caught up on his history homework. However, Ben was feeling stubborn. In his mind, the museum was practically as much his home as the big, echoing apartment he shared with his parents two blocks away. In fact, it was hard to tell the difference sometimes, because most of the apartment was littered with pairs of horns, rock samples, geology hammers, fossils, huge, heavy books, and specimen trays, just like one of the museum offices. If somebody were vandalizing *his* museum, Ben Pollock was going to put a stop to it.

He talked to two or three of the guards whom he knew and found that they had all heard about the latest happening, though sometimes the reports were not very accurate. "I'm sure glad I'm down here," said one man. "I heard a cobra got loose over there and they ain't letting anyone in."

"The fellows sure feel bad about this," said Al. "I mean, it's part of our job to see that everyone's out when the museum closes and all. And you know we do a pretty thorough job. We check the rest rooms and the storage closets and every inch of floor space. There's twenty-three acres to this museum, counting the courtyards and offices,

15

and we go over every inch. Lots of times kids—teen-agers—will try to stay in after hours. On a dare, like. But we always catch 'em—Yes, ma'am," he broke off to answer a question, "North American Birds are right through there and to your left—I say, if somebody's managed to stay in here twice in a row, he must be awful small or maybe invisible. Don't you worry, though. We'll get him if he tries it again. Everybody's really on their toes. Why, Harry Houdini couldn't get into this place now, let alone out again."

"Who's Harry Hoo-whatsit?" asked Ben, keeping his eye on a short man in a black cape who seemed to take too much interest in a fire alarm box.

"Lordy-lordy, what do they teach you kids these days? Houdini was *only* the greatest magician that ever lived. Locks didn't mean a thing to him. Hey, pal, maybe you better run along. I'm not supposed to spend my time gabbing, you know."

Al was right, Ben decided, as he said goodbye and moved away. The men were certainly paying extra attention to their jobs. Usually they were perfectly willing to chat while on duty.

During the rest of the afternoon, Ben spotted several very interesting-looking people. He watched an art student sketch one of the bronze statues by Carl Akeley in the Roosevelt Memorial Entrance Hall and listened to part of a lecture on seashells in the hall of Ocean Life. He saw a woman in a pink fur coat, a pair of four- or five-year-old twins with red hair, an enormously fat man on his knees in front of a totem pole, a scrawny girl carrying a leather-bound book as big as a dictionary, three sailors having a loud argument about which subway to take, and a young

16

woman who was talking to herself as she moved through the hall of Earth History. None of them acted particularly like a vandal.

Eventually Ben wandered into the hall of Late Dinosaurs to see if his friend Charley felt like a talk. This hall was one of the most popular in the museum and Ben understood why. No matter how often he went there, he always got a little twitch in his stomach when he looked up at the six-inch teeth, three-foot jaws, and cold, bony eye-sockets of the great dinosaur *Tyrannosaurus rex* whose skeleton was mounted there. Today, however, he could hardly get near the monster. It was surrounded by a crowd of noisy high school boys in baseball jackets. Ben walked around them and found Charley at the other end of the hall. He was answering a small girl's question about what dinosaurs ate besides other dinosaurs. At last the child went away and Ben asked sympathetically, "Some day, huh?"

"You can say that again, man. Sometimes I think it's getting worse. I had to pull a kid away from Rex, there, by the seat of his pants. His dad just stood there, and let him go under the rail. Aw, well, the kids are okay really. But some of the grown-ups. Trash? You'd think they owned the place."

"Really?" said Ben. "It usually looks pretty clean in here to me."

Charley paused to direct a man in a raincoat to Peoples of the Pacific. "Fifteen years," he went on, "that's how long I've been here. Longer than most. And in all that time I've never seen trash as bad as just this last week. Paper plates. Would you believe twice, whole paper plates? Green. And pieces of funny-looking banana on the floor. Yesterday a hard-boiled egg."

"An egg? You mean just on the floor?"

"Yes. In that corner by the window. I almost missed it. Of course, the cleanup people come through here anyway, but we're not supposed to leave anything big for them, and we have to take anything valuable to the lost and found. Who do you suppose lost a paper plate full of marshmallows and apples?"

"Charley, did you tell anybody about this?" Ben was getting excited.

"Sure, I told my wife and my brother-in-law yesterday evening. I told my friend Hooper that I ride the bus with every day. I told a couple of the guys here in the locker room, and you know what—"

"No, Charley, I mean did you tell anybody from the museum? The President or anybody?"

Charley picked up a glove and handed it back to an elderly lady. "Well, Ben," he grinned, "that old President Firth-Carpenter doesn't just come around here every day asking me did I happen to find any green paper plates. No, I didn't see him and I guess I wouldn't bother him with that if I did see him, neither."

They were strolling around the big, high-ceilinged room, watching people watching people watching dinosaurs. Outside the high windows was a gray November day, but inside Ben Pollock was a shiny red lump of excitement. "Don't you see, Charley?" he asked. "That could be very important. I mean it could have something to do with the vandals."

Charley pushed his hat back on his head and laughed. "Man, if you think vandals eat marshmallows and funny bananas to make them invisible, then you got a better imagination than I have." He looked down at Ben's crestfallen expression and said in a different tone, "Hey, I didn't mean to hurt your feelings. If you think those plates are so important, you go right ahead and watch for whoever's leaving them. I'd be obliged. And by the way, one of the other guys said he found a plate too, last week. Green. It was down on Two, I think. But I haven't heard of any others since."

"Gosh, thanks, Charley! That's a great help." Ben was halfway out of the hall when he turned around and galloped back. "Excuse me, Charley. Just one more thing. What did you mean by 'funny bananas'?"

"Huh? Oh, nothing much. Their skins were all reddish brown, that's all. Be seeing you." Ben was gone again.

By closing time, he was in the museum library on the fourth floor, where he had promised his father to pick up a book the librarian was saving for him. He hadn't found out much more about green plates, because none of the second-floor guards remembered seeing any. "It must have been one of the relief men," someone suggested.

Ben was barely in time to pick up his father's book. After the museum was officially closed, he stayed on to talk to one of the librarians, who had a daughter in his class at school. The three librarians all got ready to leave together. They were heading for the big Seventy-seventh Street entrance. However, it had started to rain quite hard outside and Ben decided to leave by the staff door from the north wing on Eighty-first Street, four blocks closer to home. He said good night to the three women and left them waiting for the elevator beside the Rare Book Room. To get to his exit, he had to go through Late Mammals, turn left in Early Mammals, keep on through Late Dinosaurs, follow a long, dead-ended corridor to a door that said Staff Only, go through the door, walk the length of the building, and descend three flights of stairs.

The trouble started when he was only halfway through Late Mammals. It was a long, high, narrow room filled with old-fashioned glass and wooden display cases. Down its center was a row of mammoth and mastodon skeletons, their tusks huge in the gloom. Now that the public were gone, the museum was lit only by a few single bulbs. Ben was walking sturdily past an extinct camel when he got the feeling he was being followed. He didn't know how he knew it, but he knew it. He whirled around, but the rows of cases reflected only silvery streetlights. An army of burglars could have hidden in the side aisles without his seeing them. He walked three steps backward, wondering whether anyone would hear him if he yelled. From quite close by came a soft but definite thump. He turned to make a dash for the door and found himself face to face with the Irish elk. Its skull grinned at him from between horns the size of snowplow blades. In ten seconds, Ben had sprinted through the next two halls, past the grand staircase, down the corridor, and was leaning against the far side of the door marked Staff Only.

One of the night watchmen came toward him around a corner. "What are you doing—" the man began, but Ben didn't let him finish.

"I think somebody was following me," he said, trying

hard not to gasp. "Back there by the mastodons." He saw the man hesitate and added, "It's all right. My parents work here." Together they pounded back down the corridor. Ben took care not to get too far ahead of the older man. He didn't much want to meet the vandal by himself.

But though they searched that whole side of the fourth floor with the watchman's powerful flash lamp, they neither saw nor heard anything.

As Ben walked home through the rain, his father's book held carefully under his windbreaker, he was very thoughtful. He used his key on the apartment front door and wandered toward the kitchen. His nose told him that fudge was being made. "Hi, Dad. Plain or walnut?"

"Peanut. Walnuts are getting too expensive. It'll be another ten or fifteen minutes yet. I hear you're going to catch the vandals."

"You do?"

"Uh huh. I ran into Dick Di Novo as he was waiting for the bus. He said you were pretty keen. Well, that's fine. You might run onto something. The police and the Protection Division don't seem to have a clue. Just don't let me catch you getting behind in your history."

Aw, Dad. What's so great about that old stuff, anyhow?"

"To tell you the truth," admitted his father, "I never could stand it myself. It's such silly little lumps of time compared to what it takes to make geology. However, I had to learn it, and you can too, or you'll be an ignoramus."

Ben knew what an ignoramus was. It was his father's way of saying "a dope." He grinned at his father and asked innocently, "Say, what was the Compromise of 1850? I have a test on it Monday."

"Get lost, shrimp," laughed his father, giving him a mock punch on the shoulder. "I haven't the faintest idea."

It wasn't until after dinner that Ben remembered to ask the question he had had in his head when he came home. "Mom, you know that kid Hernandez in my class? Remember when I went to his house and his mother fixed those brown things that looked sort of like bananas? What was it you told me they were?"

"Plantains, dear. *Plátanos* in Spanish. They're very good fried."

"Thanks, Mom." Ben didn't say anything else about "funny bananas." He didn't say anything about running away from a thump in Late Mammals, either. At least not until the New York City Police Department asked him about it.

At ten o'clock Monday morning, the principal's secretary appeared in the door of Ben's homeroom. "There's a police sergeant in Mr. Horton's office who would like to see Ben Pollock right away," she announced breathlessly. Ben walked out, leaving his whole class staring. "Hey, Pollock," called Chucky Walgren, "who'd you bump off?"

In the office of the principal, Mr. Horton, Ben found his father as well as a cheerful-looking, youngish man who introduced himself as Detective Sergeant Schafer. "Now, Ben," said his father, "I don't suppose you've seen the papers yet. This museum affair is getting a bit serious. Somebody set off the alarms in the Morgan Memorial last night, and the sergeant here says one of the night men seems to think you might know something about it. All right, sergeant, go ahead. I'm sure Ben will be glad to tell you anything he knows."

The Morgan Memorial! That was the museum's famous gem and mineral collection, containing some of the finest jewels in the world. Ben answered the sergeant's questions carefully, even though he was dying to ask a few of his own.

Yes, he had stayed after hours on Saturday. Yes, the watchman's story was right; he had reported being followed. No, they hadn't found anything. "All right, Ben, I'm going to level with you," said the detective. "There are a lot of people who would say you were just a kid who got scared of his shadow. I'm not so sure. How often are you in the museum after it closes? Were you ever scared before?"

"Well, I'm there pretty often. I mean, sometimes I do my homework in Mom's office or hang around while I'm waiting for her or Dad to get through working. And I always go to the members' programs and special evening tours. I guess you could say I'm there a lot. But I've never been scared before, except when I was *really* little and I didn't like the giant shark jaws."

Sergeant Schafer looked at Ben's father and nodded. "I guess you were right, sir. He's a pretty level-headed kid. Okay, son. Let's assume you did hear or sense something. Sometimes in police work we find people really know more about that sort of thing than they think. They hear or see something too faint or brief to notice properly. Now tell me, do you think it might have been just a tiny sound like a footstep that made you think you were being followed?"

24

Ben thought hard. He tried to imagine himself walking down that long, narrow room again, with the thin, rainy light coming in from the street. "No, sir," he said. "I don't think I heard any footstep. You're going to think this is crazy, but the first minute I thought something was wrong, I had the idea somebody was watching me from up high."

"From up high? You mean up near the windows? That's twelve or thirteen feet, isn't it? The watchman reported all the windows properly closed, but I'll check that myself. Go on. Was there anything else, or did you just hightail it?"

"No, I turned around to see if somebody was there. And I didn't see a thing, but then there was this thump. It wasn't very loud. It sounded like something soft, you know. And I think—I thought it wasn't on the floor. I remember I looked up when I heard it. And I was sure whoever it was was getting closer. That was when I got out."

"Very sensible thing to do," commented the detective. "Well, Ben, Dr. Pollock, I'll let you both get back to your work, and thank you for your time." He shook hands and started for the door, but Ben couldn't bear it any longer.

"Please, Sergeant, you never told me. What happened in the Morgan Memorial? Did they take the Star of India again?" He knew the famous sapphire had been stolen several years before and later recovered.

The detective grinned at him. "Still on the trail yourself, huh? Okay, I'll share information with you. I can use all the help I can get. The first alarm went off at 9:13 P.M. yesterday, Sunday, about half an hour after the cleaners left. I won't go into the details of the protection system on the gem collection. That's classified. But I will say there are at least three separate systems there since the Star of India was lifted that time. Normally even a fly couldn't get in without our knowing it, and the alarms are hooked up directly to the police precinct as well as to the museum's own Protection Division. All we can say is that at nine-thirteen Sunday evening *somebody* was in that room. It wasn't any flaw in the alarm system, because a second, entirely different alarm was triggered just forty seconds later. And one minute after that, the first watchmen arrived and found everything in perfect order—doors and windows sealed, systems working, nothing tampered with. Also, nothing missing and nobody in the room. Nobody. So now you know as much as I do, and I'm going to be late getting downtown. Thanks again for your help." And he disappeared down the corridor.

"Hey, Pollock, was it tough?"

"What did they want to know?"

"Did they really grill you?"

Ben's friends pushed in around him at recess, bursting with curiosity. "No," said Ben thoughtfully, "he wasn't tough at all. He was a pretty cool guy. I don't really think I was able to tell him much. But," he added, brightening up, "he said he could use my help."

3

That afternoon, Ben found the museum really humming. Although a casual visitor might not have noticed anything, it was plain that the guards were even more than usually alert. Several important officials could be seen prowling the corridors in the company of reporters or men from the Protection Division. And three men who looked quite a lot like Sergeant Schafer were keeping an inconspicuous eye on vistors to the gem collection.

Ben actually had no plans to do any detecting that day. After checking over the Star of India, still safe in its case, he stopped off briefly to watch a new filmstrip that was being shown in the Lindsley Hall of Earth History. He was on his way home to his social studies homework when he first noticed the girl with the book. Not that it was remarkable to see a person carrying a book in the museum. This, however, was a particularly enormous book, and it took Ben only a glance to confirm that he had seen the same girl and book on Saturday. That still wasn't very suspicious. However, Ben was interested in the book. It was a very big book, bound in red leather, the size of a small dictionary. It didn't look at all like a schoolbook. Even stranger, the girl wasn't carrying it under her arm or clasped in front of her, the way one would normally carry a large book. She was holding it flat in both hands. Ben decided he wanted to know more about that book. It would be more interesting to find out about it than to go home to his social studies.

When he first saw the girl, she had been going down the stairs on the Seventy-seventh Street side of the building. At the second floor she turned left into the exhibit called Men of the Montaña. It was one of Ben's favorite halls, featuring a life-size jungle, complete with trees, birds, vines, native inhabitants, and a sound recording of the screams, howls, chirps, growls, and giggles of animals in the Amazon rain forest. The light was dim and the noises were excitingly creepy.

One corner of the room was largely screened from view by green foliage and by a row of display cabinets that stood in the middle of the floor waiting to be installed. When she reached that part of the room, the girl suddenly darted between the cabinets and into the corner, so fast that Ben might never have seen her if he hadn't been watching closely. From halfway down the hall, Ben could see dimly into the place where she had gone, but only through a screen of leaves and tree trunk. He was just able to make out that she had knelt on the floor and put the book down in front of her. She seemed about to open the book when she looked up and saw him peering at her. Instantly, she made a face at him—such a horrible one that it seemed like part of the jungle scene. Then she was up and out of her corner, weaving between visitors with her book held flat in front of her. She seemed to understand that a guard would stop her if she ran, but she certainly knew how to walk fast. She was a long, thin person with wild black hair, perhaps a year or two older than Ben, and when she moved, she reminded him of garter snakes he had tried to catch at nature camp. There were fifteen yards between them when they started, but by the time the girl reached the Roosevelt Memorial, she was so far ahead that Ben knew he had no hope of catching her. He was not so far away, however, that he did not catch the glare she directed at him before she dodged out the door into the crowd on Central Park West. That girl sure was mad!

As for Ben, he was delighted. It was true that he hadn't found out anything about the girl or her mysterious book, but there was no question she had been acting suspiciously. If she had come to the museum twice, there was every reason to think she would come again. Ben walked home humming. He was making plans.

That night the museum's cafeteria was robbed. "Well, not so much robbed as turned upside down," said the caterer's representative in a newspaper interview. When Ben's friend Mrs. Tito and her assistants came in to work, they found silverware scattered on the floor, paper napkins torn from their metal holders, and bread and bananas everywhere. "Bread and bananas are the only items we don't store in the big refrigerators," explained the caterer. "They

are kept in big metal bins. We can't say how much if any-thing is missing because so much is torn up and thrown around. All I can say is, somebody must be very fond of bread and bananas. It's funny they didn't take any soda pop, though. There were cases and cases of it, all untouched. No one seems to have bothered the cash register, either."

"Bananas," said Ben Pollock to himself as he read the newspaper story the next morning. "Not 'funny bananas,' just bananas. I wonder . . ."

At four o'clock that day Ben was ready. He had on his track shoes and he had left his usual armload of books at home. Also, he had traded his windbreaker and cap for a raincoat and striped woolen ski hat. With a pocketful of fig newtons for company, he was leaning against the inner side of one of the big pillars in the main entrance hall.

Ben knew, of course, that he was taking a chance. He had no way of guessing which entrance the girl would use if she did come. However, he had taken the precaution of asking the men at the Seventy-seventh Street door and at the little street-level back entrance to watch for a skinny girl with a big book. He figured that if she was using those entrances he'd catch her next time.

In the end, he almost missed her. If he had thought his raincoat disguise was good, he had to admit hers was bril-liant. She had put on high-heeled green shoes and lipstick, so she looked almost grown-up. When she came in with a kindergarten class, she could have been mistaken for a short teacher. Ben would have made just that mistake if she hadn't been carrying the book again. There was no way to disguise it.

Ben knew better now than to follow her too closely.

He didn't want to scare her out of the museum again; he wanted to find out what she was doing there. Suspicious of her as he was, he knew she couldn't be the one who was hiding in the museum after hours. He had seen her leave yesterday, but the cafeteria had been raided just the same. Still, there had to be a connection; there just had to be.

The girl soon left the school group she had come in with and Ben had a hard time keeping his distance without losing her. His advantage was that he knew the museum inside out. He knew which halls were dead ends and where the stairways and elevators were. The girl's advantage was that she could move faster through crowds (partly because she didn't mind pushing people).

After fifteen minutes of hide-and-seek, it was clear to Ben that the girl had no particular idea of where she was going. She walked rapidly through hall after hall, upstairs and down, rarely stopping to look at an exhibit. Ben was getting even more curious. He *had* to have a look at that book she held so carefully in front of her. Then in the hall of Earth History he had a piece of luck. The new filmstrip he had watched yesterday was being shown continuously in a darkened corner. The girl stopped to join the crowd that was watching exciting scenes of volcanoes and earthquakes. Ben stopped too and wormed himself carefully near her. When he was about five people away, he was able to read the big gold letters on the spine of the book. It was called *Bottoms Up! A History of Social Drinking*, by Mary Beverage. "Huh?" Ben was so startled he had almost spoken aloud. Why on earth would a kid bring a book on beer and whiskey and so on to the Museum of Natural History? Bring it several times? It made absolutely no sense.

He had been so lost in thought that he hardly noticed when the lights went up and a new batch of people began filling the space around the screen. The girl must have spotted him when she turned to go, for suddenly she was nowhere to be seen. Then, far to his right, through a forest of legs, Ben caught a glimpse of green high heels. He turned to follow, but without hurrying. The girl had made a mistake. She was just entering the Morgan Memorial gem room. Beyond that there was nothing but Peoples of the Pacific. It was a dead end and she was trapped.

Beside a display of preserved human heads, the two came face to face. When she saw there was no exit from the room she made no attempt to get away.

Before Ben could open his mouth, she was hissing at him angrily. "What are you doing, following me around? If you don't stop I'll call the police. You stay away from me. I never want to see you again. *I hate you!*" Her green eyes glared at him and her black hair seemed to crackle.

But Ben was mad himself by now. What right did she have to mess up his museum and then call him names? "Hey, just a little minute," he began, "I want to know what you're doing here."

The girl went right on as if she hadn't heard. "You stay away from me, you hear? If not, you'll be very, very sorry. I'll get you. I'll make a little doll with pins. I'll turn you into something awful. I'll turn you into a cockroach and step on you. I'm a witch, a *bruja*. Everybody knows it. So get out of here, fast." She looked so mean that Ben took a couple of steps backward. Suddenly, she had dodged around him and was heading for the door. She walked fast, but not so fast that Ben couldn't keep up. The green shoes seemed to be giving her trouble. Ben knew that he couldn't lose her now. He matched her step for step, not quite running. In the corridor outside Peoples of the Pacific, Ben grabbed the Witch's arm. He only meant to slow her down so he could talk to her. However, she jerked away from him so hard that he was pulled off balance. As he staggered against her, she stumbled into the wall—and dropped the book. It fell to the floor with a clatter, bouncing its cover open. Ben looked down in surprise. The book was not a book at all. It was a sort of trick box made to look like a book. Inside, it was hollow. And in that hollow space was a green paper plate. There was food on the plate, some of which had spilled on the floor. Without thinking, Ben got down on his knees and started to pick up the mess. There were hard-boiled eggs, marshmallows, a partly eaten ham sandwich, some leaves of lettuce, and, yes, pieces of brown-skinned banana, *plátanos*. He looked across at the Witch, who was also on her knees, putting food back into her box as fast as she could. She had turned her back on him as much as possible and Ben saw that she was trying not to cry. She didn't look any older than he was now, in spite of her being so tall.

"Listen," said Ben awkwardly, "I'm sorry. I mean, I'm sorry about the box. You shouldn't say things like that. Besides, you've *got* to tell me what you're doing. You can't keep on messing up the museum, you know."

He waited hopefully for her to answer, but she just picked up the now refilled box and walked away. Her mouth was tight, her head was high, and she looked straight in front of her. Again, Ben followed her closely, but without touching her or saying anything. They went through the Morgan Memorial, through Earth History, across the hallway, and into Late Mammals, taking the same route Ben had taken the night of his big scare.

In Early Mammals, the Witch said without slowing her pace or turning her head, "Are you going to follow me all day, Short-and-Stupid?"

Ben clenched his fists in his pockets. "Probably," he answered. "I'll probably follow you until you stop being so mean and listen to me."

"*Me*, mean? *Me*? What do you think you are, you horrible snoop?"

They went through Late Dinosaurs and arrived at the head of the main staircase. There the girl seemed to hesitate. She cast several glances to her left, through the doorway of Early Dinosaurs. Then she turned to look at him. On her face was a despairing expression. "Please," she said, not hissing now. "Please don't follow me anymore. Couldn't you just leave me alone?"

"I don't know," said Ben. "Maybe I could and maybe I couldn't. You have to tell me what you're doing first. How do I know you aren't trying to steal something? I'm protecting the museum."

The Witch turned away down the stairs, and now she was really crying. "You *are* mean. You don't know what you're doing. He's all alone and hungry. Oh!" With a noise half gasp and half sob, she put her hand over her mouth. And though Ben followed her all the way down the stairs and out of the museum, he couldn't get another word out of her.

Ben had a great deal to think about that evening. He

should have felt excited over his discoveries, but instead, for some reason, he felt like a blue meany. Of course, he had been right about protecting the museum, he told himself. Still, if the Witch's problem was what he was beginning to suspect, she had really big trouble and he was making it worse. He had to know whether he was right, that was all. Then he could decide what to do.

After he finished his homework, he spent a long time looking through a very thick book of his mother's, filled with colored pictures. It was some help, but not much.

At dinner, he said to his father, "Dad, are you still planning to go over and work on that test you were doing? I mean, right now?"

"Well, as a matter of fact, I am. I have a new batch of samples to sort. Why?"

"Could I come along? I just want to check on something in Early Dinosaurs. It's for a project I'm doing." Ben knew that his "project" wasn't exactly what his father might think. Nevertheless, he wasn't ready to tell anybody his idea just yet.

"I suppose so. You can get to Four easily enough from my office. Just find the watchman first and tell him you're there. I wouldn't want him mistaking you for the vandal. Are you sure you're not worried about being alone again? You had a pretty unpleasant experience last time."

"No, Dad," Ben answered truthfully. "I'm not scared. And I'll take my flashlight."

At eight o'clock, Ben walked quietly into Early Dinosaurs and through into the small dead-ended room that housed Fossil Fishes. He shone his light carefully into every corner, and worked his way through the dinosaur display doing the same thing. Then he sat down on the floor and prepared to wait.

Fifteen minutes went by and Ben was getting discouraged. His father would be expecting him back soon and he couldn't check the whole huge museum.

Reluctantly, he got up to go. He'd try just one more place. He made his way through the quiet halls to Late Mammals and sat down again, this time on the base that held a fossil mammoth skeleton. All along the narrow aisle the ends of the display cabinets made stripes of light and dark. He waited five minutes without moving. Nothing. Ten minutes. Then from one corner of the room, he heard a faint but definite thump, followed by a small scratching noise. The second sound was definitely nearer. Ben felt his heart begin to beat hard. Then out of the darkness there came a sort of whimpering whine—like the sobbing, sad, and lonesome noise made by a lost child. It made the back of Ben's neck prickle coldly, but he had his answer. Or most of it. As he expected, the sound stopped the instant he moved. He got up and went over to the nearest cabinet. Unlike the newer models, the cabinets in this room stood on short legs. Ben reached in his pocket and pulled out the remains of his day's supply of fig newtons. He bent down and put them under the edge of the cabinet. It felt dusty under there, as if the cleaners didn't reach it often.

"Okay, Witch," he said to himself. "I'm not a meany now." He walked straight to his father's office without looking back.

The next morning when Ben got up, he already had a plan. He would go straight to the museum after school and hope to find the Witch. Somehow he would talk some sense into her. He didn't know exactly how he would find her, but he felt fairly sure of getting there ahead of her. He remembered he had never seen her before four o'clock, which must mean she had farther to come after school than he did. He would just work hard and trust to luck. After all, if he didn't find her that day, he would find her tomorrow.

Ben's plan became useless at three thirty-five that afternoon, when he was chatting with Al and keeping an eye out for the Witch at the same time.

"This funny business sure has everybody wrought up," Al remarked. "They're having that members' reception tonight and I hear they've taken on twenty extra guards, just to be on the safe side. The place is going to be jumping, what with them fumigators and all."

"*Fumigators?*" asked Ben. "You mean those guys you call when you've got cockroaches?"

"That's right. Exterminators. Real high-powered ones with poison gas. The museum has them twice a year, regular, on account of the danger of rats and mice or moths in the specimens. In a big old place like this you can't let those critters even get started, or you've got real trouble. The exterminating people are coming in right after the guests go. Management figures it's a good time, since the museum has to be all lit up and the elevators running and so on anyway."

Poison gas! Oh, no. Now Ben *had* to find the Witch for sure. "Are they going to do the whole place?" he asked fearfully. "Or just the downstairs?"

"The whole place. Have to. There's no way to close off just one floor. Say, what's the matter?"

40

"Al, could you do something for me? It's very important. If you see a thin, stringy girl with black hair, carrying a big red book, would you see where she goes and tell me when I come back? I know she's coming and I've just got to find her. Say, thanks a lot. I have to talk to Charley."

But though Ben made a lightning tour of the museum, giving his message to every one of the guards he knew, not one of them reported seeing the Witch or anyone like her for the rest of the afternoon.

Ben couldn't believe it. That girl *had* to come, and he knew *why* she had to come. Furthermore, if she didn't come, it landed him, Ben, with an enormous responsibility. As he left the museum with the last of the visitors at five o'clock, he briefly considered trying to stop the fumigators. It didn't seem very likely that a crew of grown men would listen to a kid with a story about a girl, a book that wasn't a book, and some unusual bananas. Al or Charley might believe him, but neither of them would have the power to stop something ordered by the museum management. Of course, there was the Museum's President. Ben had been introduced to Professor Firth-Carpenter once or twice, but he doubted that the famous scientist would remember him, even if he could get in to see him. If only there were more time! Ben knew his parents would listen to him and know what to do, but he wouldn't see them until the members' night was all over. They were taking advantage of his being away to go out to dinner and an early movie. Ben had been left with the key to the apartment, his father's membership card, half a cold chicken, and instructions to meet his parents outside the museum at nine-thirty when the program was over. It was in a rather discouraged mood that Ben went home to eat and wait for seven o'clock, when the museum reopened. He was on his own, that was all, with nothing to help him. Except, maybe, a pocketful of fig newtons.

4

It was too bad he wasn't going to hear the program that evening, Ben thought as he climbed the steps to the Roosevelt Entrance Hall. A famous underwater photographer was going to show his pictures and talk about scuba diving in the South Seas. Two and a half hours didn't seem a minute too long for what Ben had to get done, however. And it was much more important than any lecture, no matter how exciting. It was even more important than simply capturing the vandal. If only he *could* do it . . . He showed his membership card and slipped inside the high, warm hall with its columns and colorful mural paintings.

Ben knew that the plan for the evening was as follows. Members who came early could take a special guided tour of the museum, could wander on their own, or could chat in the Members' Room for the first hour. Then everyone would gather in the auditorium on the first floor to hear an address by the President, followed by the speaker of the evening. Naturally, Ben had no interest in joining a guided tour. Besides, he needed to get away from the crowd as quickly as possible. He skirted the edge of a group that was clustered around the charging African elephants—and there she was, red book and all. The Witch, with her hair in little-girl pigtails, was standing meekly by the side of a portly middle-aged man with a beard. She looked as if she were paying complete attention to the staff member who was describing the mounting of the elephants and other African mammals. Ben never knew what made her turn and stare at him almost the moment he spotted her. She made another of her horrifying faces and was off toward the end of the hall before he could even start in her direction.

This time, however, Ben had an advantage. The girl was hemmed in by a forest of adults and, push as she would, she couldn't move very quickly through the crowd. Ben, circling the edge of the group, had almost reached her by the time she broke free.

He was between her and the stairs. There was only one way for her to go. Without giving a thought to being stopped, she streaked through the far doorway, down a long connecting corridor, and into the exhibit called Man in Africa. This was one of the newest displays, not simply a large hall, but a maze of four-sided cases made to look like the grass-roofed huts of an African village. Obviously, Ben realized, the Witch hoped to lose him there by dodging in and out among them. Instead, he trotted to the middle of the floor and stood still. Voices were approaching from the corridor, but at the moment the two of them seemed to be alone in Man in Africa. "Listen, Witch," said Ben carefully. "You've got to listen to me. You don't know what's going on. The fumigators are coming—"

From two cases away there was a rustle—closer to the door than he had thought. "Listen, Short-and-Stupid." She was hissing again. "I don't care what you say. I don't want to listen to you. You're a pig, do you hear? *Puerco! Puerco!*"

As she spoke, Ben had been sidling quietly toward the sound of her voice, but it didn't work. She was off again, really running, and Ben went after her hopelessly, knowing those long, skinny legs would beat him in any race. There was a guard in Birds of the World who called out to them, but he did not follow because he was explaining the recent vandalism to a cluster of curious members. Ben's heart was pounding, but he followed stubbornly as the girl turned left into Men of the Montaña. Once he gathered enough breath to call out between gasps, "Listen, dummy. I'm only trying to help you. Honest." Then, like a motorcyclist in heavy traffic, she veered suddenly to her right and through a small door.

From forty feet behind, Ben saw where she had gone, and his heart sank. He walked slowly up to the little door. The neat sign on it was just what he had known it would be: LADIES. The cheat. The dirty cheat. Recorded sounds of the jungle seemed to be laughing at him. He saw a pair of women heading his way and immediately backed off. This was no place to hang around. But what *was* he going to do?

Ben leaned himself against a cabinet displaying poison darts and woven fish traps. He was worried and anxious, but he was also stubborn. Wildlife photographers had to be patient, he told himself. They waited for hours until the animals came down the trail. The Witch couldn't stay in there forever, could she?

Half an hour later, Ben wasn't so sure. People had come and gone through that little door, and though he had been careful to stand so he couldn't possibly be seen from inside, the Witch hadn't so much as put her head out. Now the upper floors of the museum were beginning to empty out, as the members made their way to the auditorium. The door of the ladies' room opened once more and two women walked off in the direction of the main staircase. Somewhere, someone flipped a switch, and the sounds of the Amazon jungle stopped dead.

She'll come out now, thought Ben to himself. She'll think there isn't anyone around. But she *didn't* come out. The museum was quiet, with only the hum of the ventilating system. Suddenly, Ben knew what he was going to do. He waited another minute or two, just to make sure no one else was going to come out of that door. Then he went and sat down with his back against it. He turned his head toward the crack beside the door and began to talk.

"Okay, you Witch, or whoever you are. I know you think you're smart, but I'm still here. Everybody's gone away, and I could come in there after you, but I don't want to. I just want you to listen, because it's important. I know you've been bringing food here every day and trying to hide it. I think it's for some animal, because they would have found a person. I don't know what kind of animal, but it must have been messing things up and setting off the alarms and so on." There was a sound of footsteps from behind the door, but Ben paid no attention. "Now this is the important part. I could just tell the museum about it in the morning and they'd catch you and make you stop. But it's too late for that. I tried to say it before. They're going to fumigate the whole museum tonight, right after this reception. Whatever it is you've got in here is going to be killed. Did you hear me? It's going to be d-e-a-d unless you come out of there and help me find it. You better come out right now."

Ben paused hopefully. From the other side of the door, just inches from his ear, came a snuffle. "How do I know you're telling the truth?" asked the Witch's voice. "You probably just want to scare me. Frito doesn't have any friends but me, and I *promised* I'd never let anyone catch him."

At this, Ben Pollock completely lost his temper. He jumped to his feet, pushed into the white-tiled room, and found himself face to face with the Witch. "You stupid!" he yelled. "You dummy! You don't even know when somebody's trying to help you. I even went and fed it, whatever it is. I left it some fig newtons last night. And now I'm missing a neat movie, just for you. You are the stubbornest, meanest, most stuck-up girl I ever saw—"

He was about to go on, but the girl—suddenly she didn't look like a Witch anymore—caught hold of his arm. "Did you feed him? Really? I was so worried. *Ansiosa*. For three days I couldn't. He loves fig newtons. How did you know?"

Ben suddenly felt enormously clever. "It was simple. He followed me one night when I stayed after hours. I always have fig newtons in my pocket and I figured he must have smelled food. Come on. Let's get out of here. This place makes me nervous." They went out into the now deserted Men of the Montaña.

"Poor Frito. This is where I let him loose. I thought it would be like home. I didn't know it would make such trouble for the museum."

"Like home?" asked Ben. "Say, what is Frito, anyway? I looked all through my mom's big mammal book, but I couldn't figure him out."

He had never seen her smile before. "Frito is a coatimundi."

"A coati-whaty?"

"A coati*mundi*. They live in the *selva*, the jungle. In South America."

"Oh, yeah. I remember. Sort of like a raccoon, only thinner. Listen, we don't have much time. The fumigators are coming in about an hour and a half. Do you think Frito'll come to you if you call?"

Her face clouded over. "I don't know. He is wild since he was here. Sometimes he doesn't even let me see him. But maybe, now the people are gone." She held out the book. "I have food in here, too. Come on. I think he is mostly on the fourth floor now."

"This way," said Ben. "We're less likely to meet a watchman if we use the south stairs."

Together they raced for the fourth floor, and arrived panting outside Late Mammals.

"Let's try in there," said Ben. That's where I was when he followed me and that's where I left the fig newtons."

"*Sí*. Okay. But if he's not here, we will try the little room. The one where you have to go under the shark's jaw.

I think he makes his nest there."

They had just stepped through the doorway when the lights went out. The room was suddenly filled with the spiky shadows of bones and tusks and horns. "Uh-oh," muttered Ben. "They must be saving electricity. And I didn't bring my flashlight."

His companion didn't seem worried, however. "Frito doesn't care," she declared. "He can see in the dark, and hear and smell. Now be quiet. He hides up on top of these cabinets, that biggest one in the corner. Here, Frito. Come on. *Ven aca nene, mi querido.*"

"What are you saying?" hissed Ben.

"Shh. He likes me to talk Spanish to him. *Ven aca.*" She had the box open and was holding out a hard-boiled egg temptingly.

"Say," whispered Ben, getting up from his hands and knees on the other side of the room. "He must have gotten the fig newtons. They're all gone."

"Shhh."

They waited in silence for several minutes.

Ben couldn't decide whether he was hearing things or whether there really were tiny sounds in the room. Then from the darkest corner came a rustle, and the two watchers saw street light reflected from a pair of eyes. The eyes moved and there was a thump. Ben saw a creature that seemed to be all tail and nose perched on a windowsill ten feet above their heads. There he was, the great museum vandal—two feet of striped tail, two feet of brownish body, long legs, rounded ears, black-and-white face mask, long, twitchy nose. Frito, the coatimundi.

"Here, Frito," called the girl softly. "Come on. He's

49

all right. He's just a boy. Come on."

It was a long way to the floor, and the animal seemed to want a closer look at them. He teetered for a moment on the sill. Then, instead of leaping straight down, he flung himself sideways onto the top of a wooden screen that had been placed in front of an exhibit that was being repaired. The screen, however, was only propped against the cabinet and the wall. The weight of the coatimundi sent it sliding, and with a loud crash it fell flat. Ben saw nothing but a blackish streak through the air as the terrified animal dashed from the room. "Oh, no," he groaned, "now we'll never catch him."

5

For a desperate while it seemed they never would catch Frito. They followed him through dimly lit halls and corridors, up and down stairs, in and out of dead ends. Ben realized that if the animal had tried to hide himself or outrun them they would have lost him in two seconds. I suppose he's hungry as well as scared, he thought, and that's why he doesn't disappear on us. For it was plain that the museum was a perfect hiding place for a coatimundi. Frito could not only run and jump, he could climb like a monkey and balance on the narrowest ledge like a high-wire artist. And he didn't seem the least bit tired by the chase.

Ben, on the other hand, was about worn out. It was not only Frito but Frito's owner with whom he couldn't keep up. "I'm sorry," he panted once, as they skidded around a corner together, "I can't run as fast as you do. And say, what is your name, anyway? I can't keep saying 'Witch.' "

"It's Carmen," answered the Witch. "Don't worry. Nobody runs as fast as I can. When I get older I will win all the races. And your name—what is it?"

"Ben. Okay, Carmen the Witch, you sure are fast."

It was then that Ben realized where they were. For the last ten minutes the coatimundi had been leading them around in a big circle. Now he was galloping straight up the main staircase from the third floor. Ben tried to call to the girl, but she had run on ahead of him and didn't hear.

Perhaps if he had been able to stop her, things might have been different. For Ben was right. The coatimundi had by now forgotten most of his fear and was enjoying the game. However, he was also very hungry, and the safest place to stop and eat was certainly the den he had found for himself in the little room full of fossil fishes that opened off Early Dinosaurs. If he had had time to rest a minute, shake himself, and calm down, he might have been very glad to come to Carmen, have a meal, and be carried to safety. However, the feet were still pounding close behind him. Instead of running straight to his den, he dodged left into Late Dinosaurs. In front of Frito loomed the gigantic fossil skeleton of *Tyrannosaurus rex* on its base. But the coati did not see the remains of the most terrifying monster that ever lived on earth; he saw a ladder. As nimbly as an acrobat, he ran up the enormous spine from tail to head and curled himself inside the skull.

From several yards behind in the corridor, Ben heard the girl give a shriek. "¡*Ay*! Oh, you bad Frito. Come down!" He started to run again and arrived puffing to look where she was pointing.

"Phew. What a place! Don't worry, though. He'll come down when he feels like it. At least we don't have to run anymore."

Ben was quite prepared to wait patiently for the adventurer to get tired of his strange perch. He sat down on the cold stone floor and began gropingly to arrange a plate of coati food.

At that moment, a buzzer sounded through the dark halls, loud and startling. Ben knew that it was the museum's usual closing signal. To Frito, however, it was terrifying. The space he had found inside the skull was narrow and full of strange holes and bumps. For a coatimundi it was no place to be when danger threatened. He pressed himself flat and began to scramble desperately back the way he had come. However, his groping legs failed to find the opening. Panicking, he pushed himself forward. There was a small hole in front of him and open space on the other side. He wriggled into it as rapidly as he could. Then suddenly his back feet could find nothing to push on, his front feet still pawed the air.

Twenty feet below, the Witch grabbed Ben's shoulder. "Oh, look; He is *atrapado*, stuck. In the dinosaur's *mouth!* Poor Frito. *Pobrecito.*" She was right. For the moment, the coatimundi was certainly stuck, and he opened his mouth to tell the world about it in a series of terrified squeals.

Ben jumped to his feet, really alarmed. "You don't know how bad this is," he groaned to the Witch. "The buzzer must mean the film is over and everybody's leaving. And *that* means those exterminators are going to be here any minute with their poison. *We've got to get him down now."*

The two stood facing each other among the shadows of the ancient bones. "You mean to climb up, up the back of *that?"* quavered Carmen, waving at the tyrannosaurus.

Even in his worry, Ben was shocked. "Of course not, silly. It's a fossil millions of years old. You'd break one of the most valuable things in the museum. No, we'll have to get a ladder."

"A ladder?" Carmen had to raise her voice to be heard over the buzzer. "Now who is *estúpido?"*

For answer Ben seized her by the arm and pulled her into the corridor. He heaved open a heavy door and pointed into the darkness. "Maybe you can't see it, but there's a ladder in there. A big one. I've seen them use it to clean the tops of things." Cautiously, they stepped into the large maintenance closet, stumbling a little over mops, buckets, and other equipment. The ladder, fortunately, was too big to miss.

"It is not tall enough," objected Carmen.

"Yes it is. It has another piece, an extension that you crank out of the top. And," Ben added triumphantly, "it has wheels. Come on, push."

But though it had wheels, the ladder was an old-fashioned wooden affair, enormously heavy. The two children heaved and strained at it, but the low threshold of the closet almost defeated them. Then a final shove from Carmen brought it wobbling over and its metal wheels rumbled as they hurried it along through the doorway and up to the tyrannosaurus.

At the approach of this noisy mechanism, the coatimundi renewed his squeals and his frantic wrigglings. There was no time to wait for him to calm down, however. "I'd better go up," said Ben. "I've seen how they work the extension. You hold the bottom still, okay?" He was six rungs up when he felt her hand on his ankle.

"Hey. Take him this. He doesn't know you're a friend." She was holding up a brown-skinned *plátano*.

Ben stuck it in his pocket and made for the top. Somewhere up there was a crank that would raise the next section of the ladder. He found it, but it was stiff. Whoops, no. He had been trying to turn it the wrong way. Wait till I tell Charley about this tomorrow, he thought as he cranked. He was very excited and almost light-headed. They were going to make it in time. He knew they were. He locked the crank carefully in position and went on up the much narrower and lighter upper section. The view of the hall full of fossils was amazing and the head of the great tyrannosaurus drew steadily closer. Then he was level with it and there was Frito, within relatively easy reach. All Ben had to do was take hold of the animal gently, give one good pull to free him, and the job was done.

Frito the coatimundi didn't see things that way.

He had been lured out of hiding onto a dangerous trap that fell down and nearly killed him; he had been chased all over the museum in the middle of the night; he had become terrifyingly stuck in this odd kind of tree and then frightened again by loud noises, one of which was still going on. Now he was cornered by a completely strange person who had the nerve to try to reach out and touch him. Frito did what any wild animal would have done. He snarled fiercely and bared his sharp teeth.

56

Ben drew back his hand instantly. It was plain that, food or no food, Frito had no intention of being rescued by a stranger. It would have to be Carmen, then. He started back down the ladder and heard her voice calling to him from below. The buzzer was still going, however, and he couldn't hear what she said. "He won't let me touch him," he called as soon as he was closer. His words clashed with her own repeated message. "Can't you hear? It is the *exterminadores*. They're coming." Then he, too, could hear the sound of voices and heavy equipment being unloaded from one of the service elevators. They were still on the floor below, however. Blessedly, the buzzer chose that moment to stop.

"Okay," he said as he jumped down the last few rungs. "You'll have to go up. He's scared of me."

"Up? Up there? I can't." Her face was white and she backed away a few steps.

"What do you mean, you can't? You've got to if you don't want Frito exterminated."

"You don't understand. I *can't*. I'm scared of heights. They give me the dizziness. *Vértigo*." She looked as if she were going to be sick right there.

Ben saw that this was no time to be sympathetic. "Okay, then, don't go up, if that's all you care about Frito. I guess the gas will kill him quickly. Of course, it does seem like a big waste of time, getting the ladder and all. But if you're going to be a coward about it . . ."

"*Oh!*" It was an angry gasp, but Ben had turned his back on the girl and he didn't look around. Either she would go up or she wouldn't, and there was nothing more he could do about it. Then behind him he heard the ladder

creak and a small voice said, "Since you are the brave one, you could hold the ladder."

She was still the Witch, no matter how scared she was, Ben noticed. But he held the ladder.

There was no doubt that it was a very long way up to Frito. Carmen was shaking before she had gone halfway. Ben felt it in the ladder and called up helpfully, "Try closing your eyes."

"They *are* closed." She was clinging tightly to each rung and moving very slowly. Several times she stopped altogether. Once he thought he heard a sob. He called, "Are you all right?" but there was no answer. Then Ben heard another sound—the clank of men and equipment in the corridor behind him. He realized he had no idea whether the exterminators would come into the room first and find them, or whether they would simply start filling the place with poison fumes immediately.

"Carmen," he called up desperately. "You've got to hurry. They're really coming." He saw her start to move and added warningly, "Don't look down!"

The girl was not looking down, however. She had almost reached the top and his words seemed to have forced her into action. She went up the last several rungs so fast and shakily that Ben was afraid she might really fall. It was certainly a very creaky ladder, though it was perfectly steady on its base. For the first time, he felt a twinge as he saw Carmen face to face with the monstrous skull, whose dozens of six-inch fangs grinned at her hungrily. Had he really gone up there so carelessly?

Now Carmen was leaning out from the ladder, speaking Spanish to the frightened coati. She talked to him for a

59

long minute, and Ben thought Frito must be snarling at her, too. Then she reached in between the great teeth. The ladder gave a frightening wobble as she seized the animal's front paws. Carmen gave a heave, the coati gave a wriggle, and then Frito was free and clinging frantically to Carmen's shoulder. She came down the ladder so fast she seemed to be sliding. Ben reached up to help her off and as she felt his hand on her back she asked, "Is it safe?"

"Is what safe? We've got to get *out of here*."

"I mean, am I down?"

Ben looked at her face. "Uh huh, you're down, Carmen. You can open your eyes now. Come on, we'd better go this way." He gestured toward the far end of the hall. As they reached the doorway, the lights went on. Ben looked behind them and saw four men in white suits and face masks wheel in a long metal tank with a nozzle. There wasn't much time to spare!

They galloped along the south wing and down the stairs. They were turning onto the third-floor landing when the whole museum seemed to come alive with ringing bells. "Uh-oh," Ben muttered to Carmen, "we must have set off some burglar alarm, but I don't see how." Behind them a voice called, "Hey, you, stop!" and Ben hesitated. "It's all right," he said. "They won't do anything to us."

Carmen looked at him as if he'd gone crazy. "Maybe not to you," she snapped. "But they will never catch me."

It seemed to Ben that there was nothing else to do but stick with her. "Okay, then, we'll go this way." They skipped through Primates and found another stairway on the other side. Down they went, Frito still clinging tightly to Carmen's shoulder. As usual, she had outdistanced Ben.

60

For that reason, Ben was the only one who saw what happened next. As Carmen dashed out onto the second-floor landing, she ran full tilt into a man in a leather jacket who was also making for the stairs. Carmen was half knocked down. The man tried angrily to push her out of the way. Then there was a furious squall from Frito, followed by an even more furious howl from the man. He leaped down the stairs, but he was not alone. Clinging fiercely to the seat of his pants was Frito. At the same instant, Ben saw the smashed front on the case of the special exhibit that stood just off the landing. "The Aztec gold!" he shouted. "Stop him!" He started for the stairs, but Carmen was back on her feet and way ahead of him. "Stop!" she yelled. "You bring back my coati! *Ladrón! Bandido!*"

It was only a short sprint down to the Seventy-seventh Street foyer, and Carmen made it in record time. Somewhere along the way, Frito had let go his hold and he came bounding after her with Ben not far behind.

Amazingly, the foyer was still about half full of members on their way home. Many of them stopped and stared at the sight of two children and a coatimundi chasing a grown man. It looked as if the man might simply dash out the door through the startled crowd, but Carmen got to him first. As if she were a coatimundi herself, she leaped and clung to his legs, knocking him over. Then before either of them could move, three men broke away from different parts of the crowd and seized the man. One of them was Detective Sergeant Schafer. He recognized Ben. "Well, if it isn't young Pollock. Do you mind telling me just what's going on here?"

But that was more than Ben could do right then. "He

was stealing the gold. Frito bit him," he began, panting. "No, Carmen ran into him first. We had to save Frito . . . from the exterminators . . . but he got stuck inside the dinosaur. Carmen had some food inside a book. But he wouldn't come down for it, so we had to get a ladder." He saw the expression on the detective's face and stopped. "I guess it's kind of complicated," he admitted.

"I guess it is." Schafer was interrupted by one of the other detectives.

"Look what we've got here, Dan." In his hand was a handkerchief filled with gold from the Aztec display. "Right in the jacket pocket. I guess he just intended to mingle with the crowd and walk out in the confusion. He's not giving us any trouble now."

"Okay, tell him his rights and take him in. Now, Doctor," added Schafer to a museum official who had just hurried up, "perhaps I can entrust the gold to you for the moment. Oh, and I think you may know Ben Pollock here. Do you know where I can reach his parents?"

At that, Ben interrupted. "Oh, my gosh, I forgot. They're waiting for me outside the main entrance."

"Fine. We'll let them know you're here. And now, what about your friend? What's your name, young lady?"

Carmen had been standing just behind Ben, with Frito snuggled comfortably in the crook of her arm. "My name is Carmen María Elena Moreno," she said formally. "Do I have to be arrested too?"

The detective, the museum officials, and the crowd that had gathered around them all turned and stared at her. "Well," said Schafer thoughtfully, "I hadn't planned on it. What is it you've done?"

Carmen stuck her chin out so far Ben thought she might be going to turn into the Witch again, but all she said was, "Frito is mine, and he was the vandal. I had to find a home for him and I thought he'd like it in the jungle room. I didn't know he'd cause so much trouble. But if somebody has to go to jail I hope it's me and not Frito. He hates to stay in a cage. That's why my mama made me take him away."

Schafer looked puzzled. "You mean that—that animal was the vandal? Is it possible?" he asked the museum man behind him.

"I suppose so. It's a coatimundi, you know—*Nasua narica* is the scientific name. They're very agile, very alert, very curious, and I believe they eat practically anything. It is *possible*, but it's certainly a surprise."

"But . . ." The sergeant shook his head. "What I mean is, this just isn't a very big animal. I saw that information desk the morning after, the cafeteria, too. They looked like cyclone damage. It would have been quite a lot of work for a *human being* to make that much mess. But then, I guess I'm getting confused. A bigger animal, or a person, would have had to be invisible to avoid being caught. Maybe this character is small enough to have hidden out successfully. But I just don't see how he could have done all the things he seems to have done. Or *why*. Now I *know* I'm confused."

Through a gap in the crowd, Ben saw his parents come into the hall, looking curious and puzzled about the disturbance. They're wondering where I am, he thought, and waved to them to come over. When he turned back, the museum man was talking again.

64

". . . not difficult to explain the vandalism," he was saying. "I expect the animal was hungry and the cafeteria would be the obvious place for him to go. The bird display, too. He must have found the door partially open and the feathers excited him—reminded him of wild birds he used to catch. I admit, though, the information counter has me baffled."

"Oh, but that part's easy," Ben broke in. "Don't you know the volunteers eat their lunch there sometimes when it's busy? They bring sandwiches and things, and they throw away the crusts or their apple cores. I'll bet Frito found what was in the wastebaskets and tore the place up looking for more. And I don't think he had any trouble hidding from us. There are an awful lot of dark corners on top of cases and behind columns. He can jump and balance even better than a cat, too, can't he?"

Ben turned to Carmen, who nodded. "Oh, yes. He can even walk a tightrope, like in the circus. And he can see in the dark."

"Say," interrupted Ben, "I meant to ask you. Does Frito cry? I mean, when he's lonesome maybe, or hungry?"

"*Sí*. He does. When we first got him, before he knew I was his friend, my mama used to think it was the baby crying and get up in the night. Did you hear him?"

"Yes, I heard him the night I left the fig newtons. I looked in a lot of my mom's books to try to find out what would make a noise like that, but they didn't say anything about it."

There was a stir in the crowd, which parted to let through the museum's President, Professor Firth-Carpenter. He was a cheerful-looking man with a bushy brown beard, who always seemed out of place in the business suits he wore for important meetings.

"Well, Professor," grinned the sergeant, "it looks as if we've found your vandal for you, as well as a thief. Only it's the vandal who's wearing the mask." He pointed to Frito, who stared back with his black-ringed eyes.

Carmen clutched the coati tighter and looked as if she wanted to disappear into the crowd. Ben realized that the combination of a president and a police sergeant was just too much for her. It seemed as if, once again, he was going to have to do all the talking. The President was still looking at Frito with raised eyebrows.

"Excuse me." Ben spoke louder than he'd intended, and started again. "Excuse me, Sergeant, but you haven't said yet if you're going to have to arrest Carmen. Because I just don't think that would be fair. Even though Frito was the vandal, he helped catch the thief. And Carmen *really* caught him. I think the museum ought to be very glad to have all that gold back." He was frowning as he watched both the President and the sergeant, waiting for them to answer.

Professor Firth-Carpenter shook his bushy head and smiled a slow smile. "I'm afraid I'm in over my head here, Sergeant. I don't even know what's been going on."

Sergeant Schafer was looking at Carmen. "My lord," he said, "I didn't mean to keep you in suspense." He sounded really sorry. "As far as the police are concerned, I promise you there's no question of arrest. Though, of course, it's up to the museum to decide what action it might take against, uh, Frito."

The President shook his head once again. "I'm still in

the dark, I must admit. It seems to me, however, that we've all had about enough for one night. Marcus, Charlotte, maybe you'd better take your young vandal-catcher home and see he gets some sleep. As for the young lady and her, uh, friend—Sergeant, do you think you could see them home? It's getting a little late. I suggest that everyone concerned meet in my office tomorrow at ten o'clock."

The crowd started to break up, but Carmen hung back by Ben. "But—Frito," she whispered. "What can become of him? My mama will not let me bring him home."

But that problem, it seemed, had already occurred to the sergeant. "You come along with me, young lady," he said kindly, "and I'll tell you what we'll do. We'll find a nice, warm spot in the precinct house for our stripe-tailed pal here, and I guarantee you he'll make a lot of friends on the night shift."

So Frito spent a night at the police station after all.

6

The next morning Ben, Carmen, Frito, Ben's parents, and Sergeant Schafer were gathered in the office of Professor Firth-Carpenter. It was an almost circular room because it was in one of the round brownstone towers that marked the south and west sides of the museum. Its walls were covered with strange objects brought back by the President and other presidents before him from their world travels. There was a large mechanical globe with a moon revolving around it, and, most amazing of all, there was a stuffed ostrich that served as a hatstand. The curtains, though Ben did not know it, had been woven in Peru before Columbus sailed for America, and the slanting morning sun shone cheerfully on polished wood, ivory, metal, leather, stone, and cloth. Outside the open door of

the office were crowded various members of the staff, strain-ing to catch a glimpse of the mysterious vandal. All that anyone could see of Frito, however, was a pile of brown fur wrapped in a long striped tail. After a strenuous night of exploring the police station, the coatimundi had settled onto Carmen's lap, tucked his long nose under his tail, and gone peacefully to sleep.

No one else in the room was in the least likely to go to sleep. Although the main outlines of the story were by now clear to everyone, there were still many unanswered questions. "Well, Ben," began the President, "it seems as if you're the one who can tell us the most. What made you suspect that our troublesome guest was an animal and not a human being?"

So Ben, trying hard not to look too pleased with him-self, told about his talks with Al and Charley, about their mentioning "funny bananas," about his becoming suspi-cious of Carmen, and about seeing the plantains when he accidentally made her spill what was in her box. "It seemed like a very weird meal for a person," he explained. "I mean hard-boiled eggs and marshmallows and bananas, ick. Then when I thought about it, I realized the museum was a per-fect place for an animal that knew how to hide. You'd be amazed at how many dark corners there are on top of the older display cases, and they're so high nobody can see up there without a ladder. It was Sergeant Schafer who made me think of that, actually. When he asked me about the time I was followed, he made me remember that I'd first thought whatever it was was up near the windows. And finally I remembered that I'd had fig newtons in my pocket that night—I usually do. I decided that whatever it was must like sweet things and have a good sense of smell. But I still couldn't figure out why anybody would let an animal loose in the museum, or what kind of animal it was. For a while I thought it might be a monkey, or maybe a flying squirrel. But monkeys make too much noise and a squirrel would be too small."

"Ben," broke in his mother, "I think you've just brought up another point we're all curious about. Why on earth *did* Carmen bring Frito here? And where did she get a coati in the first place?"

Everyone turned to look at Carmen, but she only wriggled further into the deep leather chair she was sitting in and said nothing. Ben saw that, amazingly enough, Carmen the Witch was feeling shy. "You said last night your mother wanted you to keep him in a cage. Was that why?" he asked helpfully.

"Yes." Her voice was small and her eyes were fixed on a ship model that hung on the wall beside her. For a moment Ben thought she wasn't going to go on, but then she added, "My uncle brought him to me. Frito, I mean. He's in the Merchant Marine. I mean my uncle." Again she looked as if she wanted to creep down behind the chair cushions. She drew a deep breath and started again. "My uncle brought Frito to me from *Sudamérica*. He bought him from a man who caught him in the jungle.

"At first it was okay. Frito was little and my mama thought he was cute. But he got bigger and he began to climb over everything, especially at night. I had a wire cage that Uncle Ramón had brought him in and Mama said I had to keep him in that all the time. But he was so unhappy —he cried like a baby. Mama said it made our baby,

71

Juanito, not sleep. Anyway, it was mean. I was getting up in the night to let him out to play in the kitchen. One night he spilled some sugar, very much. I told her I'd done it. But the night after, he broke Mama's statue—her favorite Santa Rosa de Lima. She was very unhappy with him. She said in three days I had to sell him or give him to somebody. I had to save up to buy her another Santa Rosa, too. She says her bread goes flat without it."

Carmen seemed to have gained confidence, but now she was coming to the difficult part of her story.

"I tried to take him to a pet shop, but they had cages too. I knew it was the same at the zoo. Then I thought again of the time we came to the museum from school. I remembered the big room with the trees and leaves and jungle noises. I thought he would like it there, even if not a real jungle. So I brought him that day, wrapped in my sweater. I let him go when the guard was back-turned. I saw that the men at the door didn't let people bring picnics or umbrellas inside, but they never stopped people with books. So I asked my papa if I could play with his big trick book. Uncle Ramón brought us that too.

"For a few days, it was okay again. But after that Frito began to go more and more to different places and I did not know where to leave his food. Also, I think the guards sometimes found it and threw it away right after I left it. Poor Frito. I knew he was hungry and then I heard about the trouble at the museum on the TV news. I knew it was Frito looking for food. He must have thought that stuffed rooster was a real bird. I knew I ought to catch him and take him away. Only—only I didn't know where to take him.

"And right then this boy started following me—Benjamino. I was mad! I wanted to be a real *bruja* and make a curse on him. I saw him talking to the guards—"

"You did?" interrupted Ben. "How could you?"

Carmen grinned and made a face at him, but not a really nasty one. "I can follow people, too. Sometimes you thought you were watching for me but I was watching you. I tried to look like someone else and borrowed my big sister's shoes, but you knew me and, anyway, I couldn't go fast in the high heels. I didn't pay attention to what you said when you caught me in the room with the big canoes. I was thinking about how to turn you into a bug, a *cucaracha*, and stamp on you. I didn't believe anything you said. I almost didn't believe you about the exterminators yesterday, either. They really came, didn't they?"

"Yes, Carmen, they did come," said the President, "and I can't tell you how relieved we are that you two got out in time. That gas is very dangerous stuff and the men don't see well through the heavy masks they wear. Of course, they weren't going to start until the museum was completely closed and all the staff and members had gone home. But, if you had hung around, it could have been serious. What bothers me is that you shouldn't have been there at all. We take great care to see that everyone is out before we start an operation like that. Also, you don't know what the police found out from our gold thief last night, and I think I ought to let Sergeant Schafer explain that."

The detective got up and went to stand by the windows, where he could see everyone. He made a wry face. "Well, ladies and gentlemen, I have to admit we didn't make much of a showing on this one. Not that we wouldn't have caught him in the end, but we don't yet have an established technique for dealing with coatimundis and flying saucer addicts."

"Flying saucers?" exclaimed someone in the back of the room.

"That's right, you heard me correctly. Our man's name is Walter Johanssen, and—here's another thing that may surprise you—he's a former employee of the museum. He was a temporary guard but he got fired a couple of weeks ago. It seems he was after the gold all along, but that's not why he was fired. To begin with, the other men thought he was odd. He was always talking about flying saucers and he was very suspicious of everybody. Used to accuse them of stealing his lunch, and so on. Well, maybe there was something to that, because one day he came yelling out of the locker room, claiming his lunch had been stolen again and it was some sort of animal that did it. A giant space weasel was what he said. Well, naturally enough, the shift supervisor thought he'd been drinking and fired him on the spot. He—"

"Oh, *no*," groaned Ben, slapping his forehead.

"What's the matter, Ben?"

"What a dope I am. I *knew* that, before this whole thing started. Al, the guard who works in Fishes, told me about a guy who'd been seeing things, but I never thought of asking *what* he said he saw. If I had, I'd have had the whole thing solved in one day."

"Son," said Schafer, shaking his head, "maybe now you'll understand what it's like to be a policeman. Don't ever let anyone tell you detectives look for clues. They *have* clues, nine times out of ten. They're surrounded by them. It's brains they need, so they can ask the right questions. Brains, and lots of dumb luck. I'd say you had a fair share of both. Anyway, to continue. Johanssen wanted the gold, or at least some of it, but his reason is pretty far out. He thinks certain ones of those pieces—pre-Columbian is the right name for them, isn't it?—he thinks some of them were made by men from outer space. He and some friends of his read a book that said that. They believed these gold pieces could be used in a machine to communicate with the spacemen back in their home galaxy. They wanted the spacemen to tell them how to save the world, or something. No harm in that, I guess, except they decided their machine wouldn't work without the pre-Columbian gold.

"After Johanssen got fired he planned to use the forthcoming members' night to his advantage. He had a stolen key to one of the storage closets. All he had to do was come in with the members, hide in the closet, and wait. He knew, of course, that all the alarms would go, but he timed his move for the period when the Seventy-seventh Street foyer would be full of members leaving. All he would have had to do was run down one short flight of stairs and mingle with the crowd on the way out. It just *might* have worked. That is, if the coati rescuers hadn't come along and, um, got their teeth into him. I say it was a very fine piece of work, and I believe Professor Firth-Carpenter here will agree with me when I say the museum is very grateful to all three of them."

The President seemed about to stand up and make a speech of thanks, but a small, red-faced man pushed his way forward. "That's Dr. Harrison Carson," whispered Ben to Carmen. "He's in Insects."

"Now, just a minute," said the man. "We're all pleased that the thief has been caught, though I'm sure the police would have found him anyway. But there's another matter I want taken up. What about the damage this animal has done? What about the ruined display, the cafeteria, the information desk? Most of all, *what about my Ruthie?* I still haven't found her."

"Now, Dr. Carson, now, Harrison." It was Ben's mother who went up to the angry little man and put a soothing hand on his shoulder. "We know you thought very highly of Ruthie, and she certainly was a remarkable tarantula. But I'm afraid you'll just have to accept the fact that Ruthie is no longer with us."

"Not with us? What do you mean?"

"Harrison, I may be a specialist in Asiatic ruminants but I remember a little basic mammalogy. Unless I'm very much mistaken, *Ruthie was eaten by Frito.* Coatimundis will eat almost any small creature and they're quick enough so they don't worry about tarantula bites."

"Eaten? My Ruthie eaten? Oh, my!" Dr. Carson seemed too astonished to say anything else and sat down suddenly on the arm of a nearby chair.

Carmen, however, had half turned and was staring at him. "Excuse me. Sir? Is it one of those big hairy spiders? Those *tarántulas?* You *like* them? Please, my uncle Ramón —the boat he sails on is a banana boat. They find those spiders often in the bananas. If you want one, I am sure he could get you a big, fat one. I will ask him. It's bad when you are missing a friend."

Dr. Carson looked at her in surprise. "Why, that's very decent of you, child. Very decent. Only fair, too. I accept.

What nobody recognizes," he continued, turning to leave the room, "is that the tarantula is much misunderstood. It is clean, companionable, adaptable, quiet, and remarkably intelligent. You'd think a group of people who call themselves scientists would be less narrow-minded . . ." His voice faded away down the corridor.

"Well," resumed the President, smiling, "now that old Harrison has had his say, I think that about takes care of everything. Of course, there's no question of our pressing charges against Miss Moreno. There was some damage done, but I understand the Peabody Museum at Harvard has agreed to trade us a new jungle fowl for some fossil fishes and everything else was minor, though I'm glad Dr. Carson can't hear me say it. The important thing is that the gold artifacts, which are literally priceless, have been returned undamaged. And now I think the time has come for us all to get back to running a museum and to let these young people go with our sincerest thanks. In fact, as a special token of our appreciation, I hereby appoint Ben Pollock and Carmen Moreno honorary life members of the museum. Our thanks to you, too, Sergeant, though I understand you can't accept a membership. Come back and see us soon, all of you. I know Ben will do that, at least." He stood up and began shaking hands all around.

Carmen and the Pollock family were seen to the door with renewed thanks. On the way, they met Mr. Jackson, the man who had been repairing the bird display with Dr. Di Novo. "Hey, Ben," he said grinning. "Will you let me out of my promise?"

"What promise?"

"I said I'd punch the vandal for you when you caught

77

him. I guess that snout is too long and twitchy to punch properly. Maybe I could just pat him instead."

Frito graciously allowed himself to be patted, but Ben noticed that Carmen had turned quiet again. She hardly said a word and just held tightly to Frito. He had finished his nap and was now sitting up on her shoulder, twitching his long nose at the strange smells and generally showing off.

"Wow!" said Ben, as the five of them at last broke away and headed down the corridor, "life members! Isn't that great, Carmen? I bet we're the youngest life members the museum ever had. Usually you have to be old and rich. Wait till you get home and tell your mother."

He was still chattering on and Carmen was still silent

when his mother said, "Ben dear, haven't you forgotten something?"

"Me? No, Mom, I've got my jacket right here."

"No, I don't mean that, for once. You said to Carmen, 'Wait till you tell your mother.' But what does she have to tell her? She helped catch a thief, it's true, but I suspect Mrs. Moreno is going to be much more concerned over the fact that Frito can't go on living in the museum. I don't think the police precinct can give him a home, either. If I were Carmen, I'd be wondering what to do about that."

Ben looked at his new friend and saw that, far from sharing his excitement, she was now looking very down indeed. Then he looked back at his parents, who were holding hands and smiling.

"Well, Ben," said his father, "don't you have any suggestions?"

Ben looked at his parents again, then at Carmen, and suddenly he understood. "Say, Carmen," he said, "listen." For some reason he was almost shy now himself. "I think what they mean is—I mean how would you like it if—if Frito came and stayed with us? It wouldn't be as good as having him yourself, I know, but you could come and visit him anytime. We have high ceilings and lots of bookshelves for him to climb, and I guess he'd have a hard time breaking my dad's rock samples. I'll give him fig newtons every night." He stopped there because he was suddenly all tangled up with a girl and a coati. "Wow," he said when she had finished hugging him. "I guess it's all right then. I always said I'd get the vandal, but didn't know he'd come to live with me."

ABOUT THE AUTHOR
• • • • • • • • • • • • •

Georgess McHargue, a graduate of Radcliffe College, is a former editor of children's books. She gave up that career in order to devote all of her time to writing. She has since had numerous books published, all of them receiving wide critical acclaim. Some of her recent books are *THE IMPOSSIBLE PEOPLE, THE MERMAID AND THE WHALE* and *HOT AND COLD RUNNING CITIES.* Ms. McHargue lives in Cambridge, Massachusetts, where she devotes much of her time to research in folklore and mythology.

ABOUT THE ILLUSTRATOR
• • • • • • • • • • • • • • • • •

Heidi Palmer was born in Switzerland and has lived in Europe, Canada and the United States. She received her B.F.A. at Pratt Institute, and has illustrated magazines and several children's books. She enjoys working in her vegetable garden, tending her flowers and her animals, and collecting, among other things, old children's books. Ms. Palmer makes her home in Old Greenwich, Connecticut.

ABOUT THE BOOK
• • • • • • • • • • •

The text for this book was set in Baskerville typeface with display type in Cooper Black. The illustrations are pen and ink drawings and the book was printed by offset.